CRICKET in Times Square

Chuck Jones

From the original story by George Selden

Ideals Publishing Corporation

Milwaukee, Wisconsin

ISBN 0-8249-8074-3

In a sunny Connecticut meadow Chester Cricket was bounding from rock to rock. He was looking for something good to eat.

Suddenly he stopped, his antennae quivering. Just in front of him stood an open picnic basket.

"Liverwurst!" he exclaimed. He hopped into the basket and looked around. "Yum! Liverwurst *and* roast beef!"

Chester began to eat. He didn't notice the thunder clouds rolling in. He didn't notice the lightning slashing through the sky. The wind blew harder. CRASH! Down came the picnic basket lid. Chester was alone in the dark.

He heard footsteps running toward him.

"Wow! It's coming down hard!" a voice shouted.

"Grab the basket! Run for the train!"

Chester felt the picnic basket lifted up. "Where are they taking me?" he wondered. He didn't know he would soon be on a train to New York City, traveling far from his beautiful country meadow home.

Tucker Mouse sat at the opening to a drain-pipe in a New York City subway station. He was watching a young newsboy, Mario Bellini, who was calling out, "Get your late papers... music magazines...all the latest editions...!"

Tucker sighed. "The poor kid might as well go home. No one's buying anything." Suddenly Tucker saw feet approaching. He ducked back into the drainpipe.

The feet were Paul's. Paul was a train conductor and one of Mario's regular customers. Paul bought a music magazine and hurried off.

"Wait, Paul, your change," Mario called after him. Paul paid no attention. He knew Mario needed the extra money.

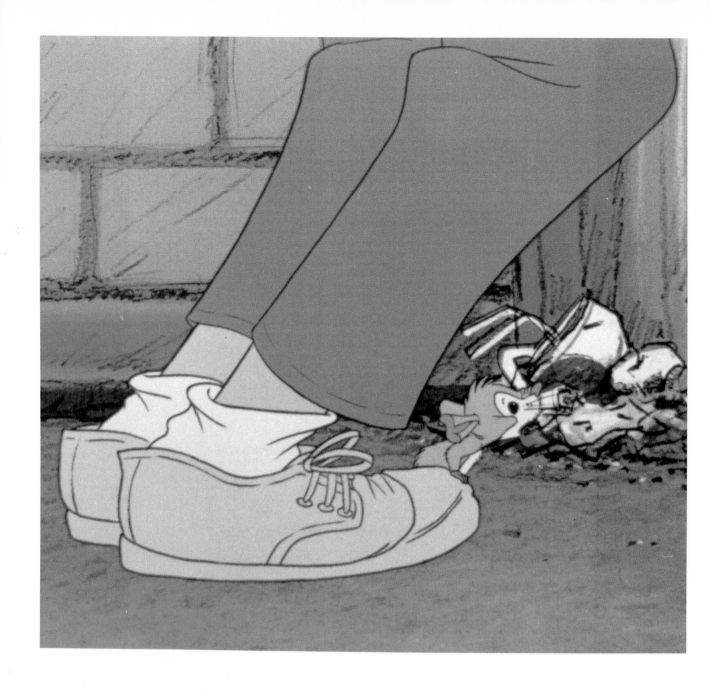

Just then Mario heard a chirping sound that seemed to come from a pile of rubbish. "What could that be?" Mario wondered. Carefully he sorted through the pile.

"Why, it's a cricket!" Mario said. "How did he get here?"

Tucker Mouse, who was still watching by the drainpipe, edged closer so he could see, too. He had never seen a cricket before, because country crickets don't live in New York City subway stations.

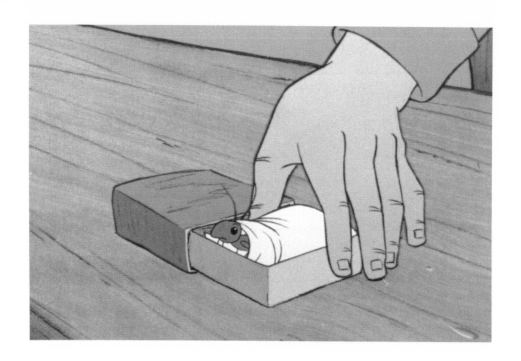

Mario fitted some tissue into a matchbox. "This will make a nice home for you," he said, tucking Chester in.

"Chirp! Chirp!" said Chester, just as Mario's father and mother came to take Mario home.

"Mario, what's that noise?" asked Mrs. Bellini.

Mr. Bellini looked into the matchbox. "Why, it's a cricket," he said.

"It's a bug! It's got germs! Throw it away!" cried Mrs. Bellini, stamping her foot. She almost stamped Tucker Mouse, who had edged even closer.

"No, don't throw him away," said Mr. Bellini. "Crickets are good luck."

"That's right, Mama," said Mario, as he stroked the little cricket. "It's not just a bug. Please, Mama, let me keep him for a pet."

Mr. Bellini decided. "Mario can keep him here in the newsstand," he said.

"He won't cause any trouble, Mama," Mario promised. "Goodnight, cricket," he whispered. "I'll be back in the morning."

After Mario and his parents went home, the coast was clear for Tucker Mouse to climb up to the newsstand.

"Psst! Hey you!" he whispered.

Chester Cricket looked out over the top of his matchbox.

"Hi! I'm Tucker Mouse," said Tucker. "Who are you?"

"I'm Chester. I'm a country cricket," he said. "But where am I now?"

Tucker was just beginning to tell Chester about the subway station, when a large orange cat leaped up on the newsstand counter.

"Look out, Tucker! A CAT!"

"Don't worry," said Tucker. "This is my best friend, Harry Cat."

Chester was surprised. In the country, all the cats and mice he knew were enemies. Things were certainly different here in the city.

"Chester can make music," continued Tucker. "Show him, Chester."

Chester chirped some soft, musical chirps. Harry began to purr. Tucker said, "You two

sound wonderful together. You should stay with us, Chester. We'd all be friends. Won't you stay?"

Chester looked around at the busy subway station. He missed his beautiful Connecticut meadow. "Well, I'm not sure," he said. "Mario's mother doesn't like me — she thinks I've got germs..."

"That doesn't mean anything," said Harry. "She's just worried. The whole Bellini family is worried because business isn't good, and Mario isn't selling enough magazines."

"Well, maybe I will stay," said Chester, "if I can help."

Early the next morning, Mario dashed to the newsstand with some breakfast for Chester.

"Liverwurst!" said Chester. He quickly ate up every bit.

Tucker and Harry watched enviously from the drainpipe. They liked liverwurst too. Mr. Smedley, another regular customer, stopped by the newsstand for a music magazine.

"Why, a cricket!" he said, peering into the matchbox. "Will you chirp for me, cricket?"

Chester began to chirp.

"He's a talented musician," Mr. Smedley said. "I have something for him — something I found in China long ago. Wait until I come next time; then you'll see it."

Several days later, Mr. Smedley returned, carrying an elegant cricket cage.

"Thank you, Mr. Smedley," said Mario. "It's just right for my cricket."

"There's a story about crickets I'd like to tell you," Mr. Smedley said. "It's a Chinese story. Would you like to hear it?"

"Yes!" said Mario.

Tucker and Harry, down by the drainpipe, wanted to listen too. "I just love stories," said Tucker.

Mr. Smedley began:

"Long, long ago, there were no crickets. In that long-ago time lived a very thoughtful man who was kind and wise and spoke only the truth. His name was Hsi Shuai. Wicked people did not like to hear the truth, so they decided to kill him.

But the high gods loved Hsi Shuai. To protect him, they turned him into a cricket. Since that day, all crickets sing songs that everyone loves ...because most of us love the truth."

When the story was over, Chester softly chirped himself to sleep. Harry hadn't moved. Tucker murmured sleepily, "What a lovely story. I had no idea that telling the truth could be so beautiful..."

Every evening after the newsstand closed, Tucker, Harry, and Chester sat together and talked. They became very good friends. In the daytime, Chester watched the people in the subway station. He listened to Mario selling magazines. He listened to the radio. He nibbled on liverwurst.

One night, when the subway was quiet and when Chester was dozing, Tucker Mouse scurried

over to the newsstand carrying cupcakes with
candles in them. Harry followed with a picnic
basket.

"Ready, Tucker?" asked Harry.

"Ready!" said Tucker.

"SURPRISE! SURPRISE!" they yelled as
Tucker struck a match and lit the candles.
"Look! We've even got sodas with *ice!*"

Chester jumped up in his matchbox.

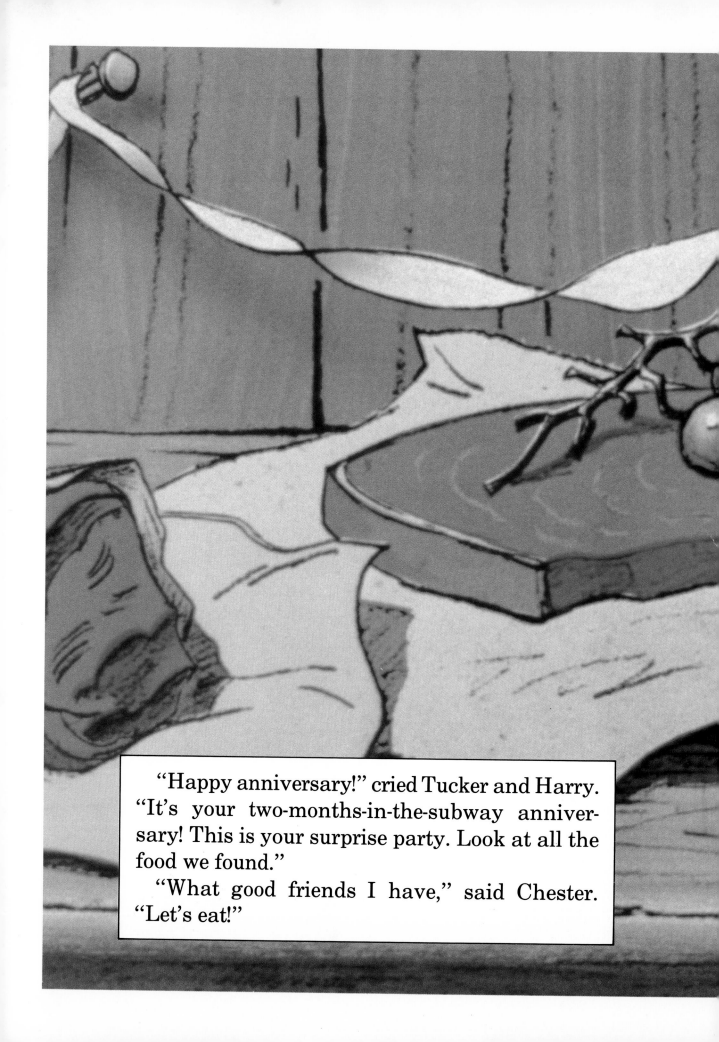

"Happy anniversary!" cried Tucker and Harry. "It's your two-months-in-the-subway anniversary! This is your surprise party. Look at all the food we found."

"What good friends I have," said Chester. "Let's eat!"

"We need some music," said Tucker, turning on the radio. The music came out softly, and Harry began to purr. Then Chester decided to play along too.

Harry and Chester looked up, startled. Chester wasn't playing his ordinary chirps; he was playing tunes like the ones on the radio.

"Why, I didn't know you could play like *that*," said Tucker.

"It's lovely," echoed Harry.

"I didn't know I could play like this either," said Chester. "I never heard radio music in the country, and I thought I'd try to play it myself."

Then Chester began to play other radio tunes. Harry and Tucker danced and leaped to the music.

No one noticed when Tucker's tail swept the cupcakes with the burning candles into the wastebasket.

Tucker's nose began to twitch. "I smell smoke!" He stopped dancing. "Look out!" he shouted. "The wastebasket is burning! It's burning!"

Tucker and Harry tried to smother the fire with stacks of magazines. Then people came with fire extinguishers. Soon the fire was out.

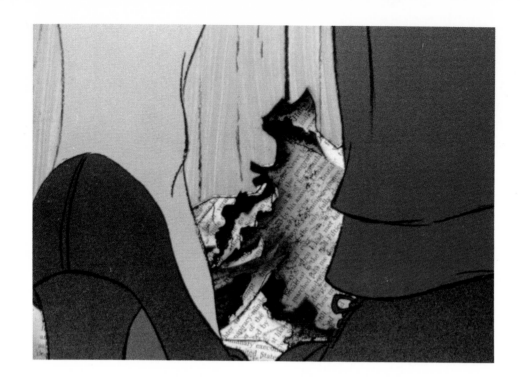

In the morning, Mario and his parents saw what was left of their newsstand.

"We are ruined!" sobbed Mrs. Bellini. "It's the cricket's fault! He asked in his pals. Out he goes! Don't try to argue with me, Mario."

Chester did feel a little responsible. To cheer himself up, he began to play a sad, sweet tune.

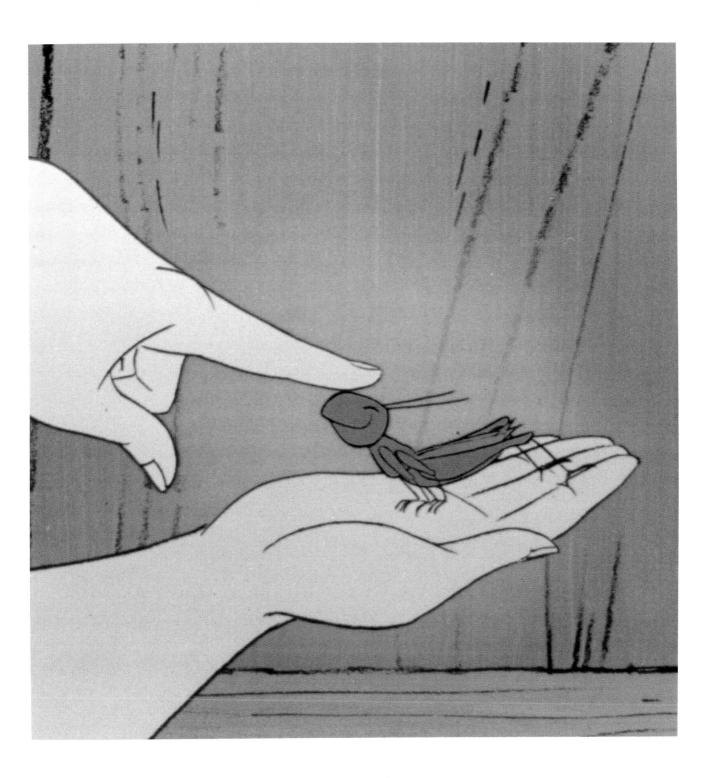

Mama Bellini stopped yelling and began to listen. Chester played louder. He played music that made Mrs. Bellini think of warm summer days and of hills and meadows in the country. Even Tucker and Harry had never heard Chester play so beautifully. Mrs. Bellini stroked Chester and said, "He can stay a while longer. No cricket who plays such lovely music would start a fire."

The newsstand was repaired, but business still wasn't good. Then Tucker had a plan.

"Chester is a very talented musician," he said. "If Chester plays during the daytime, people will stop to listen. Then Mario will sell them magazines, and the Bellinis will get rich, and EVERYONE WILL LIVE HAPPILY EVER AFTER!"

"What a fine idea!" said Harry.

"I'll learn more songs," said Chester. He settled down by the radio. After he learned one tune, he began another. The newsstand filled with song.

One day while Chester was practicing, Mr. Smedley came by.

"Beautiful!" he said. "What station are you listening to?"

"It's our cricket," said Mrs. Bellini proudly. "Our wonderful cricket!"

"Amazing!" said Mr. Smedley. "The whole world should know about this cricket."

Letters to The Editor

TO THE MUSIC EDITORS
THE NEW YORK NEWSPAPERS

Mr. Smedley wrote to every New York City newspaper, telling them about Chester. Many people read the letter. They came to the newsstand to hear Chester play.

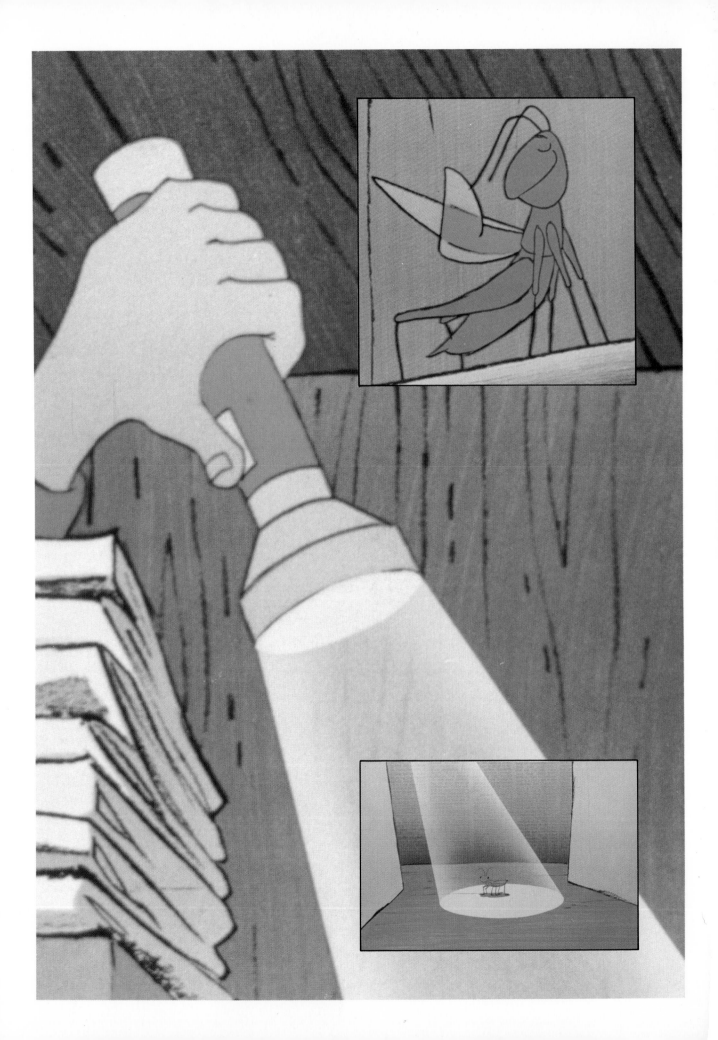

Mario made a stage out of two cigar boxes. He used a flashlight for a spotlight. When he turned on the flashlight, the crowds quieted down, and then Chester played his music. When Chester finished, the audience cheered. Then they bought magazines from Mario. Every day, Mario sold all his magazines.

Tucker kept count of the magazines Mario sold. His plan was working! "We could sell even more magazines if we had them," he said proudly.

After months of concerts, Chester, Harry, and Tucker met for a special breakfast at the drainpipe. "Thanks, Chester," they said. "You have saved the Bellini family business. Let's eat and celebrate."

Chester looked at all the food his friends had brought. He was very happy. He was tired, too, because he had been working so hard.

"Thank you," he chirped. "This is a lovely party. But I must get right to sleep. I am *so*

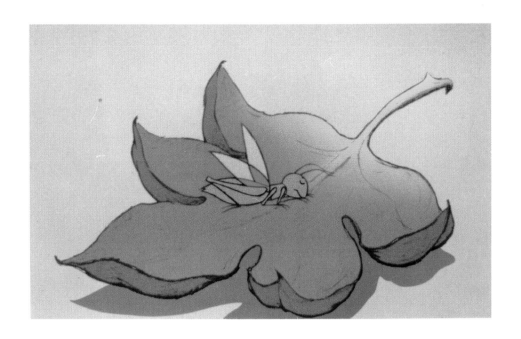

sleepy. And tomorrow night is the big weekend concert."

As he spoke, the wind whisked a beautiful yellow, gold, and red leaf into the station. When Chester saw it, he remembered that outside, autumn had come. The leaf landed on the floor in front of him. Chester hopped on top of it and soon he was asleep on the leaf, dreaming of golden leaves, green meadows, and pumpkin fields and rows of corn.

The next morning Chester said to Harry and Tucker, "It's time for me to leave the city and go back to the country where I belong. I'm a country cricket. After tonight's concert, I'm going home."

Tucker was sad. "We'll miss you," he said. "We hoped you would stay."

"But we understand," added Harry. "A subway station isn't the place for a country cricket."

"One thing worries me, though," said Chester. "What about the newsstand? If I don't play my music, will the crowds still come? Will Mario sell lots of magazines?"

"Don't worry about that," said Tucker. "Our newsstand is so famous now it will probably stay famous forever."

Chester's last concert was scheduled for Friday evening, when the station was busiest. So many people came to hear Chester that the police had to keep the aisles to and from the subway train open with ropes.

Chester wanted his last concert to be his very best. He played his most beautiful songs. Soon Chester's melodies filled the train station. People stopped rushing around and joined the listening crowd at the newsstand. Outside, drivers stopped tooting their horns and pulled over to the side of the road so they could listen. The trains stopped, so the engineers and passengers could listen. Soon everyone in the whole city was listening. For a few minutes, the city was peaceful as a country meadow in the evening.

At last Chester stopped playing and lay down on his leaf. Mario stroked him gently and then put him in his cage.

"I know you want to go home," Mario said softly. "I want you to go home because I love you and I want you to be happy." Chester looked up and chirped softly.